For Mum and Dad

Odd Dog Out
Copyright © 2016 by Rob Biddulph
All rights reserved. Manufactured in China.
No part of this book may be used or reproduced in any manner whatsoever without written
permission except in the case of brief quotations embodied in critical articles and reviews.
For information address HarperCollins Children's Books, a division of HarperCollins
Publishers, 195 Broadway, New York, NY 10007.
www.harpercollinschildrens.com
ISBN 978-0-06-236726-6
The artist used a pencil, some paper, a scanner, Photoshop CS5, a Wacom Tablet,
and a Cintiq 6D Art Pen to create the digital illustrations for this book.
19 20 21 22 23 SCP 10 9 8 7 6 5 4 3 2 1
❖ First U.S. edition, 2019
Originally published in the UK by HarperCollins Publishers Ltd.

ODD DOG OUT

Written and illustrated by

Rob Biddulph

HARPER
An Imprint of HarperCollinsPublishers

For busy dogs
a busy day

of busy work
and busy play.

Swimmer . . .

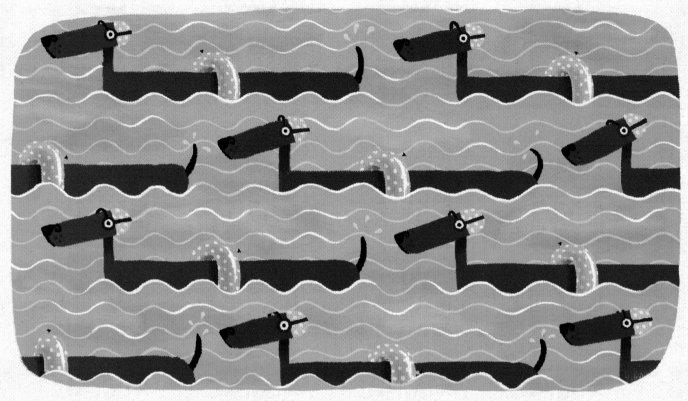

sailor . . .

soldier . . .

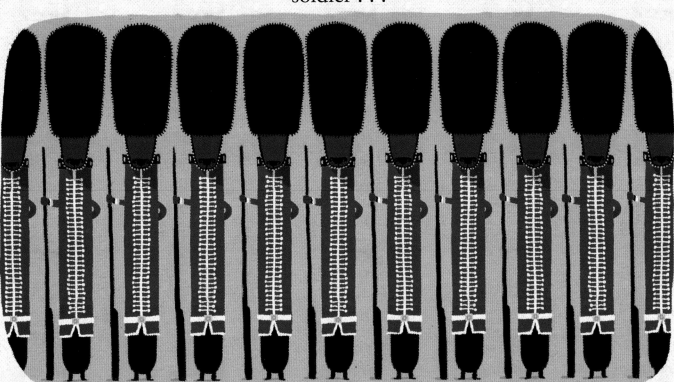

scout . . .

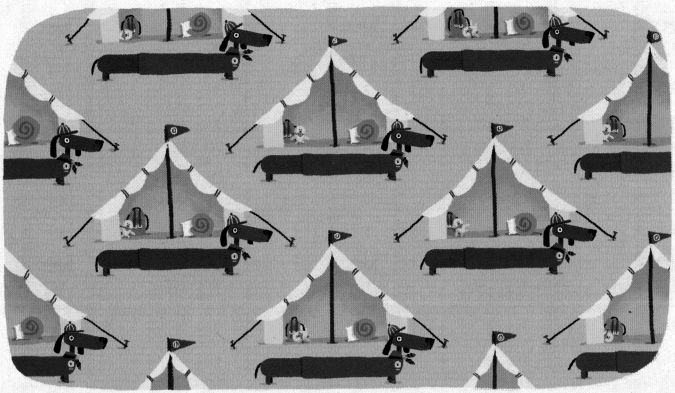

They all blend in. No dog stands out.

But wait. Look closer. Can you see
one dog behaving differently?

Someone on this
busy street

is dancing to a
different beat.

When they
fly high . . .

this dog flies low.

When they say "Kick!" . . .

this dog says "Throw!"

It's very sad
(cue violin),

but this small dog
does not fit in.

"It's true," she sniffs. "I've tried my best,
but I'm not made like all the rest.

And that's why I've made up my mind
to leave this town, my home, behind."

On
her
own
and
out of
place,

she
sighs
a sigh
and
packs
her
case.

Through winter . . .   springtime . . .

summer . . .

fall . . .

to mountain tall,

she walks till she can walk no more.
Is this the place she's looking for?

"Well, bless my bow-wow, can it be?
A hundred others just like me!

But wait. Look closer. Can you see
one dog behaving differently?

Somebody this
afternoon

is whistling a
different tune.

Here's something she knows all about:
a classic case of "Odd Dog Out."

"Poor thing," she says, "I feel for you.
I once was an outsider too."

"Oh, not at all. You've got it wrong.
I really feel like I belong.

I love to stand out from the crowd!
And so should you. Stand tall. Be proud."

She tilts her head.
She pricks her ear.
And suddenly
it's crystal clear. . . .

"That dog is right.
It's plain to see
there's nothing wrong
with being me."

Her little tail begins to wag. She smiles a smile and grabs her bag.

"I'm sorry, but I have to fly."

"Good luck, my friend!"

They wave goodbye.

From night and moon to light and sun, her journey home has just begun.

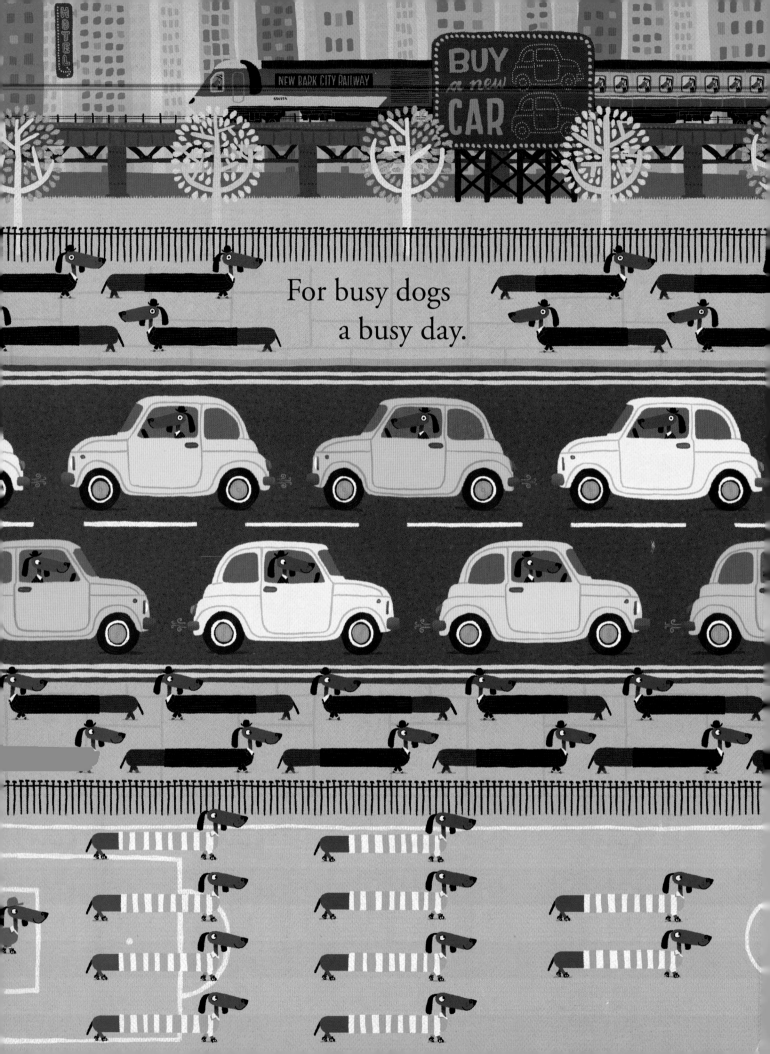

For busy dogs
a busy day.

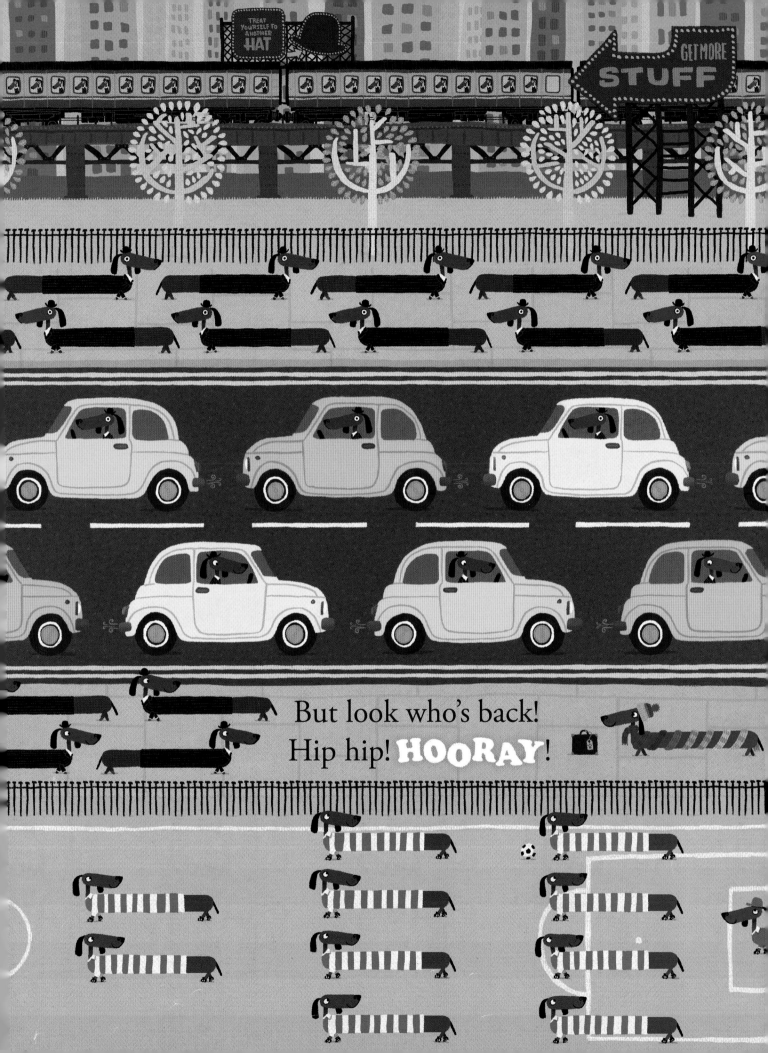

But look who's back!
Hip hip! **HOORAY**!

They **cheer**! They **clap**! They **whoop**! They **shout**!
"We've really missed our Odd Dog Out!

You've made us all appreciate
that being **different**'s really great!"

It's true! Look closer. Can you see more dogs behaving differently?

Each one a doggy superstar . . .

So blaze a trail.

Be who you are.